Louie The Buoy

David Billings

AuthorHouse™
1663 Liberty Drive
Bloomington, IN 47403
www.authorhouse.com
Phone: 1-800-839-8640

First published by AuthorHouse   7/16/2010

ISBN: 978-1-4520-3010-4 (sc)

Library of Congress Control Number: 2010909284

Printed in the United States of America
Bloomington, Indiana

This book is printed on acid-free paper.

authorHOUSE®

Grinspoon Institute for Jewish Philanthropy

380 Union Street, Suite 200

West Springfield, MA 01089

Attention: Mark Gold, Director

Nancy Billings

2475 South Bayshore Drive #1

Miami FL 33133

305 775 3470

nancybdesigns@yahoo.com

August 18, 2011

Dear Mr. Gold,

I am so thrilled to have all my grandchildren signed up for your awesome program.

I am also thrilled to be sending you a copy of my husband's book Louie the Buoy to be considered for your organization. My husband wrote this book for our grandchildren's enjoyment and has ultimately been enjoyed by many children in our neighborhood and local Jewish Day school, Temple Beth Am.

The story, as you can see is a lovely tale about friendship and doing good for others while also having beautiful illustrations. Louie the Buoy has been a wonderful book for ages 2-8 and we are confident that your organization would be thrilled with the responses from the recipients.

Please let me know if you are interested in acquiring books for your organization.

Sincerely

Nancy Billings

THIS BOOK IS DEDICATED TO MY
ENTIRE FAMILY WHO HAS ALWAYS
ENCOURAGED ME TO STEP OUT OF
MY BOX AND TRY SOMETHING NEW.

HI, I'M LOUIE. I AM A BIG RED BUOY. I AM 12 FEET TALL AND 6 FEET WIDE. BEING BIG MAKES IT EASIER FOR BOATS TO SEE ME.

I HAVE A BRIGHT LIGHT ON MY HEAD AND A LOUD HORN STRAPPED TO MY SIDE. MY LIGHT HELPS BOATS SEE ME AND MY HORN LETS BOATS HEAR ME WHEN IT IS DARK OR THE WEATHER IS BAD.

I LIVE IN THE WATER NEAR A BUSY HARBOR.

A HARBOR IS A PLACE FOR BOATS TO STAY WHEN THEY ARE NOT BEING USED. A HARBOR ALSO PROTECTS BOATS WHEN THE WEATHER IS BAD.

My job is to help small boats and big ships travel in and out of the harbor safely.

CRUISE SHIPS ARE ONE OF THE BIG BOATS THAT I HELP. THEY CARRY LOTS OF PEOPLE.

CRUISE SHIPS ARE HAPPY SHIPS. THE PEOPLE ON THEM ARE ON VACATION AND THEY ALWAYS SMILE AND WAVE TO ME.

Cargo ships are another type of big boat that I help. They carry almost everything that we use each day.

Some of the things cargo ships carry are cars and furniture. But the most fun things are toys.

$\mathcal{I}$ ALSO HELP COAST GUARD SHIPS AND POLICE BOATS TRAVEL IN AND OUT OF THE HARBOR. THEY PROTECT THE HARBOR AND KEEP EVERYONE SAFE WHEN THEY ARE IN THEIR BOATS.

ANOTHER ONE OF MY FAVORITE BOATS IS FREDDIE THE FISHERMAN'S BOAT. FREDDIE IS THE CAPTAIN. WE QUICKLY BECAME GOOD FRIENDS. HE WAVES TO ME EVERY TIME HE GOES OUT TO FISH.

WHEN FREDDIE COMES BACK AT THE
END OF THE DAY HE TOOTS HIS HORN
AS SOON AS HE SEES ME. HE ALWAYS
BRINGS BACK LOTS OF FISH.

EATING FISH HELPS KEEP PEOPLE
HEALTHY.

ONE MORNING FREDDIE THE
FISHERMAN WENT OUT FISHING JUST AS
THE SUN WAS COMING UP. HE LIKED TO
GET AN EARLY START.

WE WAVED TO EACH OTHER AS HE WAS
LEAVING THE HARBOR.

A FEW HOURS LATER THE WEATHER CHANGED AND DARK GRAY CLOUDS REPLACED THE BRIGHT YELLOW SUN.

BOATS STARTED RETURNING TO THE HARBOR.

Soon the winds picked
up and rain began to fall.
I helped guide the boats as
they returned to the harbor.

THE RAIN WAS BECOMING HEAVIER. I COULD BARELY SEE ANYTHING.

I REALIZED THAT ALL THE BOATS THAT WENT OUT THAT DAY HAD RETURNED, EXCEPT FOR FREDDIE THE FISHERMAN.

I WAS WORRIED THAT FREDDIE MIGHT BE LOST.

$\mathcal{I}$ TURNED ON MY BIG LIGHT AS BRIGHT AS POSSIBLE SO IT WOULD BE EASIER FOR FREDDIE TO SEE ME.

I ALSO STARTED BLOWING MY HORN SO FREDDIE COULD HEAR ME IF HE COULDN'T SEE ME.

A FEW MINUTES LATER I
HEARD A *TOOT TOOT* AND THERE
WAS FREDDIE THE FISHERMAN
COMING BACK TO THE HARBOR
WEARING HIS SHINY YELLOW
RAINCOAT AND HAT. HE WAS
SAFE.

THIS MADE ME FEEL VERY GOOD. IT IS A WONDERFUL FEELING TO BE ABLE TO HELP A FRIEND ESPECIALLY WHEN THEY ARE IN TROUBLE.

SOON THE RAIN STOPPED AND THE STARS CAME OUT.

NOW I COULD SLEEP AND GET READY FOR TOMORROW'S WORK.

SEE YOU AGAIN SOON

VISIT ME @ LOUIETHEBUOY.COM

Louie

LaVergne, TN USA
28 July 2010
191117LV00002B